SMALL WALT
AND
MO THE TOW

Story by **Elizabeth Verdick**

Pictures by **Marc Rosenthal**

A PAULA WISEMAN BOOK
Simon & Schuster Books for Young Readers
New York London Toronto Sydney New Delhi

SIMON & SCHUSTER BOOKS FOR YOUNG READERS
An imprint of Simon & Schuster Children's Publishing Division
1230 Avenue of the Americas, New York, New York 10020
Text copyright © 2018 by Elizabeth Verdick
Illustrations copyright © 2018 by Marc Rosenthal
SIMON & SCHUSTER BOOKS FOR YOUNG READERS is a trademark of Simon & Schuster, Inc.
For information about special discounts for bulk purchases, please contact
Simon & Schuster Special Sales at 1-866-506-1949 or business@simonandschuster.com.
The Simon & Schuster Speakers Bureau can bring authors to your live event.
For more information or to book an event, contact the Simon & Schuster Speakers Bureau
at 1-866-248-3049 or visit our website at www.simonspeakers.com.
Book design by Lizzy Bromley · The text for this book was set in Archetype.
The illustrations for this book were rendered in Prismacolor pencil and digital color.
Manufactured in China
0718 SCP
First Edition
2 4 6 8 10 9 7 5 3 1
Library of Congress Cataloging-in-Publication Data
Names: Verdick, Elizabeth, author. | Rosenthal, Marc, 1949– illustrator.
Title: Small Walt and Mo the Tow / Elizabeth Verdick ; illustrated by Marc Rosenthal.
Description: First edition. | New York : Simon & Schuster Books for Young Readers, [2018] |
Summary: Walt the snowplow learns that, while his work is very important, there are some things he
cannot do without the help of his new tow truck friend, Mo.
Identifiers: LCCN 2018000431| ISBN 9781481466608 (hardcover) | ISBN 9781481466615 (eBook)
Subjects: | CYAC: Snowplows—Fiction. | Wreckers (Vehicles) —Fiction. | Friendship—Fiction.
Classification: LCC PZ7.1.V4615 Sm 2018 | DDC [E] —dc23
LC record available at https://lccn.loc.gov/2018000431

FOR THE BEST "CREW" EVER:
OLIVIA AND ZACHARY
—E. V.

FOR ALL THE LITTLE GUYS
—M. R.

A bitter blizzard. A snowbound town.
GET READY, PLOWS!

One by one, engines rumble awake.
Two by two, headlights wink on.

There's Small Walt with a big load of
ice-melting salt, his driver Gus at the wheel.

"We're mighty tough snow-fighters," says Gus. "Let's roll!"

Walt's engine surges:
We're Gus and Walt.
We plow and we salt.
We clear the snow
so the cars can go!

Plow, push the drifts!

Spreader, scatter salt!

Wipers, swish the slush!

VARROOOM-VROOM
VROOOOOOM!

Tires, turn that snow to mush!
Varrooom—vroom—vroooooom!

On a lonely two-lane road
slick with ice, Walt slows.

A little car slips and slides.
Walt's lights shine: *Danger, danger!*
Gus grips the wheel tightly. "That driver needs to get home."

Whoa, the car pitches into the ditch.

Walt stops. *Errrr-errrrrnt.*

Gus says, "The ditch is deep. So is the snow."

Oh no, Walt's engine groans. Gus gets his gloves.

GRRRRRR, goes Walt. *Stay here, Gus, stay here.*

Walt's plow swings up; his plow drops down.

We've traveled far.

Let's scoop that car!

"Now, now," says Gus. "Plows only scoop snow."

He hops out and disappears into the ditch.

Walt waits. And waits.

My plow is tough,

but it's not enough.

Blinding snow blocks Walt's view. *What to do? What to do?*

Then, a sound in the distance . . . *brumm-brumm-humma-hum.*
A tow truck?

Gus must have made the call.
Walt watches, his wipers *swish-swishing*.
The truck pulls up; its engine hums hello:
I'm Mo. Mo the Tow.

A lady in a bright blue coat steps out.
"We can give you a hand," she says.

In howling wind and falling snow,
Gus lends a hand—and shoulder.

Brrrr. So *cold.* The wild wind howls. The snow falls faster.
Gus and the car's driver climb into Walt's cab to warm up.
Walt's heater blasts: *Whooooosh!*
"Now," Gus says, "let's see what Sue can do."
Walt's engine hitches: *Who?*

The lady in blue—*Sue*—hops
into the tow truck.
Mo looks ready to roll.
All Walt can do is wait.

Uh-oh! The snowdrifts are too high—the ice is too slick!
Mo's tires can't get a good grip. *Sliiiiiiip!*
Whoa, grrrrrumbles Mo, we can't go!

Walt to the rescue!

His engine revs: *Vrrrum, vrrrum*, here we come!

We're Gus and Walt.

We plow and we salt. . . .

Walt's plow pushes away the snow. *Scoop-scooooop!*

His spreader scatters salt: *switch-twist, switch-twist.*

Clear that muck,
or truck gets stuck!

Soon the snow is piled high.
Walt's engine heaves a huge sigh.
Mo *rrrrr*umbles:
You cleared the snow.
Now we can tow!
Here we go!

Mo and Sue back up with a shrill *beep-beep-beep!*

Sue works the boom and hook.

Clang-a-clank!
Clunk-a-clunk!

Walt's lights shine brighter.
His engine urges Mo to *go-go*-GO:
When we need a tow,
we call on Mo.
We can depend
on our new friend!

Mo *humma-brum-brums* and

PULLS,

LUGS,

HAULS . . .

Slowly, *slowly*, the car crawls up the ditch.
Whumpa-thumpa-bumpa-bump!

"Thanks to you *all*,
I'll get home!"

RUGGA-BRUM-BRUM

HUMMAROOOM!

RuggaRooom, goes Walt.
Brumma-hum, goes Mo.
Nose-to-nose, the two trucks make a ruckus:
Rugga-brum-brum, HUMMAROOOM!

"Let's get back on the road again, snow-fighter," says
Gus, as he rolls down the window and waves good-bye.
The snow whirls and flies.

Walt's engine booms:
Gus, Walt, Mo, and Sue.
What a crew—what a crew!